T0303806

IMAGINARY FRIENDS

26 WHIMSICAL FABLES FOR
GETTING ON IN A
CRAZY WORLD

MELANIE LEE • ARIF RAFHAN

Marshall Cavendish
Editions

This book was previously published in 2014 as *Imaginary Friends: 26 Fables for the Kid in Us* by MPH Group Publishing Sdn Bhd. This new edition features updated text and all new full-colour illustrations.

Published by Marshall Cavendish Editions
An imprint of Marshall Cavendish International

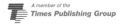

A member of the
Times Publishing Group

Other Marshall Cavendish Offices:
Marshall Cavendish Corporation. 99 White Plains Road, Tarrytown NY 10591-9001, USA • Marshall Cavendish International (Thailand) Co Ltd. 253 Asoke, 12th Flr, Sukhumvit 21 Road, Klongtoey Nua, Wattana, Bangkok 10110, Thailand • Marshall Cavendish (Malaysia) Sdn Bhd, Times Subang, Lot 46, Subang Hi-Tech Industrial Park, Batu Tiga, 40000 Shah Alam, Selangor Darul Ehsan, Malaysia.

Marshall Cavendish is a registered trademark of Times Publishing Limited

National Library Board, Singapore Cataloguing-in-Publication Data

Name(s): Lee, Melanie, 1979- | Arif Rafhan, illustrator.
Title: Imaginary friends : 26 whimsical fables for getting on in a crazy world / text: Melanie Lee; illustrations: Arif Rafhan.
Description: Singapore : Marshall Cavendish Editions, [2018]
Identifier(s): OCN 1042276404 | ISBN 978-981-4828-47-5 (hardcover)
Subject(s): LCSH: Fables, English—Singapore. | Wit and humor.
Classification: DDC S823—dc23

Printed in Singapore

To Darren and Christian,
my biggest encouragers in telling stories
— Melanie

To my bandmates; Suhana, Mya, Hamka and Avicenna.
Thank you for expanding my one-man band.
— Arif

CONTENTS

FOREWORD

Dear reader,

As a child, I was convinced that toys, stationery and even food led secret, dramatic lives that unfolded when humans were not around. I refused to eat vegetables because they were family members of my secret alien friend Captain Veggie, who was planning to rescue them at any minute. The pink Little Twin Stars water bottle I brought to school was a prim and proper lady called Janet. My pencil box, with multiple compartments that could be snapped open by pressing colourful buttons, provided safe refuge for my flag erasers that a class bully stabbed incessantly with a mechanical pencil.

I wrote these stories when my son was just an infant, and I was waking up every three hours to feed him. During those bleary moments in the wee hours of the night, I started to think about what my earliest childhood memories were. This inevitably led me to nostalgically revisit this motley crew of colourful companions that contributed towards many a school teacher describing me as "dreamy" and "absent-minded".

I realised how much I missed being able to whip up a back story of any object that came my way. I suddenly developed a burning desire to come up with "imaginative stories", the kind of far-out fiction that I had not really written since I was ten. In my hyper-sleep-deprived-state, I churned out these trippy tales which ended up featuring my childhood imaginary friends in modern-day PG-rated fables in adulting.

This is not a book for children, but it is definitely inspired by my childhood. While these fables are meant for grown-ups, it is my hope that they also remind you to see the funny and the whimsy in this crazy adult world through child-like lenses.

Yours imaginatively,
Melanie

A

is for

ANNIE THE
AMBITIOUS APPLE

Annie the Ambitious Apple was a shiny red apple from Rosy Creek Orchard. She outshone all the other apples in Mr Farmer's apple basket.

Mr Farmer was sending her to compete in his town's Best Apple Competition in a few days. It was an honour that Annie was pleased, if not a little smug, about. After all, she had beaten over a hundred ripe apples to represent Rosy Creek!

Because Mama Tree had always told her she was the prettiest one in the orchard, Annie was quite sure she would win first prize. She smiled at the thought of all the farm fruits fawning over her blue ribbon.

The day before the competition, as Annie sat beaming inside a wooden bowl in Mr Farmer's kitchen, she suddenly heard a squeaky "Hello" coming from below her. She looked down and saw an orange worm smiling at her.

"What a slimy stalker," Annie thought to herself as she pretended not to notice the worm.

However, the worm would not stop saying "Hello". She had no choice but to acknowledge its presence.

"Do I know you?" asked Annie, annoyed.

The worm bowed politely. "Oh, don't mind me, Miss Annie. I just wanted to thank you for your cosy hospitality while I was just a wee little hatchling."

Annie had no idea what the worm was talking about. Maybe he had caught some bug from the mad cows at the neighbouring farm.

"I don't think you should stick around the kitchen too long. Mrs Farmer doesn't like your kind around here," Annie said dismissively, and pretended to focus her attention on a motivational fridge magnet so she would not have to continue the conversation further. She sighed in relief as she saw the worm crawl out the kitchen window.

The next day, as Mr Farmer was about to place Annie into a Styrofoam box, he noticed a small black hole at her bottom.

"Oh blimey, not another bad apple," Mr Farmer muttered as he threw Annie into the trash bin. He hastily went back to the orchard to grab the next shiniest apple from the basket. This time round, Andrew the Annoying Apple, Annie's brother from the same tree, was selected.

Andrew was absolutely gleeful about becoming the last-minute replacement. He stuck his tongue out at the remaining apples in the basket, who were doomed to oblivion at cut-throat supermarket aisles.

"So long, suckers! Now it's my turn to shine," he sneered at them.

Andrew performed pretty well during the Best Apple Competition. In fact, he snagged third place for Rosy Creek Orchard and the yellow ribbon was pinned on the kitchen fridge. After that, Mrs Farmer sliced Andrew up and made a crusty apple pie.

MORAL OF THE STORY
Never be too smug about success or good fortune for you'll never know when the shit will hit the fan.

B

is for

BERTIE THE BURNT-OUT BUTTERFLY

When an unremarkable caterpillar transforms into a beautiful butterfly, this metamorphosis is typically regarded as a positive change.

However, such a drastic transformation from a blob-like cocoon to a fluttering kaleidoscope of colours could also be a bit overwhelming for introverted creatures such as Bertie.

Bertie was burnt-out from the sudden human praise and admiration for his newfound beauty. He found all this meaningless and hollow. It disturbed him that his peers had appeared to forget their humble beginnings and seemed more interested in flirty fluttering and posing with pollen.

Bertie also wasn't a fan of the daily groups of screeching schoolchildren who visited the butterfly enclosure he lived in. They always gave him migraines. He longed for those uninterrupted days of cruising along a dewy leaf in the silence of dawn, or meditating within the warm solitude of the old cocoon.

One day, a particularly loud group of schoolchildren visited the butterfly enclosure. The noise became so unbearable that Bertie had to find the nearest resting spot to catch his breath. This was how he ended up being on the nose of 10-year-old Willie.

All of Willie's classmates screamed in delight. All of the butterflies screamed as well (but you wouldn't be able to hear them if you were human). They had been warned never to make any physical contact with humans unless they wanted to risk getting smashed like a mosquito or pinned down as a specimen.

Despite all the commotion, Bertie didn't want to move from Willie's nose because he was just so exhausted. He just didn't care anymore.

Willie gently picked Bertie up by his wings and placed him in a small plastic container with holes on its cover.

"Hey Mr Butterfly, I'm going to sneak you out of here," Willie whispered to him as he slipped the plastic container into his bag. Bertie liked the fact that Willie wasn't as loud as the other kids and he made little effort to resist such comfortable captivity.

After a restful three-hour nap in Willie's bag, Bertie was finally released. He found himself in a small garden with a small bush of flowers, an apple tree and a vegetable patch. Living in the garden were a few bees, ladybirds, fruit flies and Bessie the Bashful Butterfly, who generally preferred not to talk more than 10 minutes a day.

Bertie lived happily ever after.

···

MORAL OF THE STORY
Being a social butterfly is not for everyone.

···

C

is for

CHUCKY THE CLEVER
CALICO CAT

Life was good for Chucky the Clever Calico Cat. Every morning and every evening, Mrs Lim fed him cat food, and the rest of the day he was free to roam around other people's houses in the neighbourhood.

It was a wonderful anthropological study, these domestic visitations. It fascinated him to no end how each home had a specific smell and feel, so much so that he felt like he was flitting in and out of different worlds.

The house he enjoyed visiting the most was the grey, cube-shaped bungalow five doors down from Mrs Lim's place. Inside, everything was black or white. Chucky appreciated the clean structural lines of the place. Most of the other homes he visited were cluttered and had no sense of aesthetic consistency.

The owner of this tasteful house was Mr Grey, a semi-retired angel investor who only ever wore a) a black turtleneck with white pants or b) a white turtleneck with black pants.

In the middle of this living room sat a beautiful white Steinway grand piano. Chucky loved to sit by Mr Grey's feet while he played selections from the *Great American Songbook* — George Gershwin, Cole Porter, Irving Berlin — all the greats of yesteryear.

In fact, Chucky spent so much time listening to Mr Grey that he eventually figured out how to read music notes and play the piano himself. On the days that Mr Grey went to the city for business meetings, Chucky would practise playing the piano with his nimble paws. He was fond of the catchy beats of bossa nova and began to compose his own samba ditties to amuse himself.

Meanwhile, Mr Grey was puzzled as to why there were scratch marks on his piano. At first, he told his cleaner off for over-polishing the ivory keys, but when the scratch marks persisted despite the cleaner using a soft flannel cloth, Mr Grey decided to install a security camera in his living room. Imagine his shock when he viewed the footage of Chucky improvising on the piano with *The Girl from Ipanema*!

But instead of loading this video onto YouTube and earning a lucrative revenue from a video that was sure to go viral, Mr Grey became gripped with a jealous rage over Chucky's obviously superior musical talent.

He took a knife to give himself multiple (but superficial) cuts on his arms and face, and marched over to Mrs Lim's house.

"Your cat is psycho! He attacked me for no rhyme or reason," Mr Grey yelled.

Horrified, Mrs Lim brought Chucky to a vet to have him euthanised. She didn't want to risk having Chucky hurt anyone else.

The week after Chucky was buried in Mrs Lim's backyard, Mr Grey bought himself a new black grand piano.

MORAL OF THE STORY
Sophisticated people with good taste do not necessarily have good hearts.

D
is for
DAN THE
DOWDY DURIAN

"You're on the front page of the tabloids today," Priscilla the Perfectionist Peach Publicist informed Dan the Dowdy Durian as he was getting his thorns sharpened at the beauty parlour. She showed him the story.

FRUITY TIMES EXCLUSIVE

Dan the Dowdy Durian's Thorny Brush with Dating!
"I just want someone to love me for who I am on the inside."

Poor Dan the Dowdy Durian! While his acting career has been soaring, his love life is an absolute flop right now despite such a warm personality. Oh girls, you have got to look past those spiky green thorns and body odour! I mean, he didn't ask to be born like this, did he?

As you might already know, Dan was recently spurned by Miss Sally the Sweet Strawberry. While they did go on three dates, she is much too afraid of getting punctured by him to take their relationship any further. It's a pity, as Sally really does enjoy talking to Dan and says that, intellectually, they're just like two peas in a pod. But who are we kidding? Have you seen the two of them together? Dan's at least 30 times her size. We can't blame Sally for getting the jitters about becoming jam with him around!

We recently had a chat with Dan on what qualities he's looking for in a soulmate. It turns out that ol' Danny Boy here just wants "a fruit who is tough on the outside but soft on the inside" — just like him!

Aww, Danny, I'm sure there's a fruit out there who is a perfect fit for you! In fact, top-notch dating consultant Jenny the Jackfruit just told us the other day that she thinks that Dan could just hit it off with pop singer Pamela the Perky Pineapple. We love Pam's positive energy, and like him, she hails from exotic tropical lineage, so they are definitely shippable! Can you already imagine them on a romantic beach vacay together? We sure can!"

"Excellent work, Priscilla, this is just the kind of fake news I need," Dan said as his berry beautician finished sharpening the last thorn. He looked across where Jenny was sitting on a lounge chair getting a coconut-oil polish.

"Sweetie, the tabloids are off us. We can go for brunch at Blossoms today and everyone will just think I'm getting dating advice from you."

....

MORAL OF THE STORY
Always treat celebrity gossip as fiction.

....

E

is for
ELLY THE
EGOTISTICAL ERASER

No one dared to mess with Elly the Egotistical Eraser at The Pencilbox — rub her the wrong way, and she would erase your existence away.

In short, she was your typical rude rubber who never considered how the pencils felt about having their markings obliterated for no rhyme or reason.

Her bullying erasures became so bad that Peter the Pious Pencil once staged a Be Nice to Nibs demonstration and wrote, "RESPECT OUR WORDS, RESPECT OUR ART" on his banner. Elly branded him a despicable vandal and rubbed out his words so hard that Pat the Pleasant Paper tore. This incident was later referred to as The Paper Massacre.

However, things were changing at The Pencilbox. All the pencils except Peter had been mysteriously removed. In their place were now pens and correction fluid — all brand new and giving disdainful looks to Peter and Elly.

"Ewwww, you both are, like, so 1980s and, like, so need a bath," snorted Percy the Perverse Pen, a sleek black gel ink pen from Japan. He had a strange fetish for poking Elly, who now looked diseased with small black dots all over her.

However, the real thug was Loratio the Loutish Liquid Paper. He liked to flick his toxic fluid on anyone who came close to him, and was notorious for deliberately seeping on pen nibs so they would not work anymore. Because of the strong hold he held over the pens, he became the de facto supreme leader of The Pencilbox.

One day, Elly the Egotistical Eraser went sobbing to Peter the Pious Pencil after Loratio flicked some fluid at her.

"I'm so sorry I was such a tyrant before! But life with these jerks is unbearable. Is there any way we can get out of this?"

Peter pitied Elly and decided that he would show her his escape plan that he had sketched out on a tiny piece of paper (a remnant of dear Pat, RIP). Apparently, just further down Study Table Avenue was The Pencilcase, a roomier, retirement sort of place where the other pencils were staying in.

"But you have to promise that if I take you along with me, you will erase all your nasty bullying habits," Peter said firmly.

Elly promised, and that very night, they popped out of The Pencilbox and made their way to The Pencilcase where they now lead a carefree existence with the pencils and a few chirpy crayons.

Meanwhile, the pens at The Pencilbox haven't noticed that Elly and Peter are gone. They're too busy trying to survive under Loratio's terrifying regime.

....
MORAL OF THE STORY
If office politics get too ridiculous, just get out.
....

F
is for
FREDA THE
FRIENDLESS FROYO

All the desserts had been giving Freda the cold shoulder ever since she was voted #1 dessert last year by the customers of Sweet Tooth Café.

It was befuddling to her why they were so resentful. It was just a silly, inconsequential title for marketing, and it was not as if she'd backstabbed any other dessert to get to the top (unlike Brigitte the Bitchy Brownie, who had once kicked Wally the Whimsical Waffle out of the freezer).

The chilly treatment became too much for Freda to bear. Even the toppings were tepid when she tried to make conversation with them. She approached Ingrid the Insolent Ice Cream, the long-time ring leader of the desserts squad, to attempt some kind of truce.

"Hey Ingrid, could you let me know why you are so angry with me? I haven't done anything to you, have I?" Freda asked helplessly.

Ingrid gave her a long cold stare that made Freda shiver.

"That's precisely it, Freda. You did nothing," Ingrid spits out. "I can't believe some random health fad has actually made you popular. You don't even taste nice; you're essentially just a diluted, putrid version of me."

"Yeah, Freda," Brigitte the Bitchy Brownie added with an air of aggressive hostility, "You don't know how much you've messed things up around here. Ingrid had been #1 at Sweet Tooth for the past ten years. And you... you almost didn't even make it to Sweet Tooth two years ago. You were just the token addition to have around in case a few fitness freaks decided they would have a dessert that tasted like crap so they wouldn't feel guilty."

Freda was crushed. She had used to admire both of them for their endearing popularity as classic desserts. Now, she finally saw Ingrid and Brigitte for who they really were: two insecure, self-absorbed sweets who only cared about staying at the top.

Freda realised that she had to strategise. Firstly, while at work, she began to casually spread rumours amongst the gossipy toppings that Ingrid actually came from a dodgy factory in China that used toxic gelatine. Secondly, she would openly bring up the high sugar level of a brownie, and how such a nutritional travesty went against the nationwide health campaign to prevent diabetes.

It was not long before Sweet Tooth Cafe became a popular froyo parlour.

MORAL OF THE STORY
Never retreat if others attack you
out of jealousy.

G

is for

GRETA THE
GROUCHY GRAPE

Greta the Grouchy Grape found it stifling being stuck with the rest of her siblings 24/7. She also hated how they were addressed collectively as The Bunch by the other fruits in the fridge's bottom drawer.

"Goodness, don't they know we all have our own names?" Greta would sulk to herself. It didn't help that all the other grapes were zesty and earnestly persisted in trying to cheer her up.

"Aw, c'mon sis, isn't it great that we're so closely connected to each other like this?" Gary the Giggly Grape would chirp. "Most fruits have to be on their own, but we get to have so much fun together!"

Gary's idea of fun was Greta's source of migraines. The Bunch (*sans* Greta) loved to sing. More specifically, they adored cheesy oldies and had no qualms belting them out tunelessly. Everything from *I Heard it Through the Grapevine* to *Days of Wine and Roses* were massacred by them. Greta would tell them that they were just torturing the other fruits in the fridge, but her siblings would just laugh at this and called her a sour grape.

And it was true, all that sulking and complaining was making Greta a pretty nasty fruit. By the time The Bunch was taken out from the fridge to form part of a fancy cheese platter, she had become brown and shrivelled while the rest of the bunch remained perky and purple.

Greta was plucked out and thrown into the bin. The bin didn't smell great, but she was looking forward to some much-needed me time.

However, the bin also housed a group of religious raisins who were preparing themselves for the end of the world. They gravitated towards her with open arms.

"You are our prodigal sister. We love you as God loves you," they chimed in unison.

Greta the Grouchy Grape rolled her eyes and told them to shut up. She rolled herself all the way down to the bottom of the bin so that she could finally get her me time.

The last few hours of her life in solitary trash ended up being Greta's most contented period of her life. Even when the rubbish removal truck came, she hardly sulked.

MORAL OF THE STORY
Sometimes, it is better to be alone rather than be stuck with undesirable company.

H
is for
HERMAN THE
HOPELESS HIPPO

Herman the Hopeless Hippo was the bane of Mama Hippo's life. He woke up only in the afternoon, he was always rolling around in the mud and he just couldn't be bothered to find himself a mate.

"Herman!" yelled Mama Hippo every morning. "Can you get up now and stop being such a filthy slob? How will you ever find yourself a nice girl at this rate?" Mama Hippo was envious that most of her river fellowship friends were already grandmothers. She longed for the day she could cuddle and coo over a cute little baby hippo once again.

Herman would pretend not to hear her repetitive nagging and sunk his head deeper into the mud. The more Mama Hippo berated him, the more he immersed himself in inertia.

It was not that he was a hedonistic hippo. In fact, once upon a time, Herman had been deeply in love with Heather the Hot Hippo, and they'd almost become mates for life. However, before their romance could have blossomed to its full potential, Mama Hippo made a slip to Heather about how she expected Herman to take on multiple mates. "I want many grandkids," she had declared.

Heather was a well-travelled and sophisticated hippo who found such an arrangement unacceptable. Soon, a bitter conflict between them ensued, and it eventually involved a vicious mud-slinging session between the old and young female hippos.

Herman was terribly torn between the two women in his life, so much so that he would secretly cry into the mud when no one was looking. Heather sensed his turmoil and decided to be the bigger hippo. She told him that she would never want to come between him and Mama Hippo.

Heather broke up with Herman and moved to another river. Her departure broke his heart. In her absence, he found little motivation to do anything remotely productive or social. Mama Hippo hated to see her son so aimless and unmotivated, but she was secretly relieved that he was spared from being mated to such an aggressive female.

However, six months after they had broken up, Herman had been reduced to a sorry state. Sometimes, Mama Hippo even had to gather grass for him because he couldn't be bothered to find food on his own. One day, it finally dawned upon her that there was only one way she could get Herman back on his feet again.

"If your heart is still with Heather after all this while, you better get her back," Mama Hippo told him.

For the first time in a long time, Herman's head emerged from the mud with a toothy smile. He lumbered out of the mud pool and gave his mother a big slobbery kiss.

With that, Herman set out to find his true love, and Heather was finally reunited with her hippo soulmate on her terms.

MORAL OF THE STORY
If you fall for a mama's boy, you will
need to have a lot of patience.

I

is for
IGNATIUS THE
IMPECCABLE IGUANA

Ignatius the Impeccable Iguana was like the Ryan Gosling of reptiles. He was suave and muscular, and had a remarkably friendly personality for his species.

Every time he strutted around the swamp, even the rather ferocious female monitor lizards would suddenly get rather shy and giggly in his presence.

"Oh, Iggy is such a hunk. Too bad he's not my type," they'd whisper amongst themselves as he sauntered past them with an endearing wink and a dazzling smile.

All the creatures in the swamp appreciated his charming disposition and glistening emerald skin. Everyone wanted to be around him. Everyone wanted to hear what he had to say.

One day, a human explorer left behind a book titled *Iguanodon: A History & Taxonomic Study*. Besides being extremely good-looking, Ignatius was also exceedingly intelligent and devoured the book, both figuratively and literally, for knowledge and dietary fibre, within an hour. He started to feel inadequate compared to his distant ancestors.

For one, the iguanodon had been a spectacular giant that could switch easily between moving on two limbs and four limbs. It also had a five-fingered hand, complete with a spiked thumb. How could Ignatius ever match up to all these superior physical features?

Ignatius started getting cranky about the injustice of being born a genetically sub-par reptile and snarled at anyone who tried to talk to him. He stopped filing his claws. He hardly ever checked his reflection by the river anymore. What was the point? He would never become a dinosaur.

Soon, everyone in the swamp called him Ignatius the Irritating Iguana and avoided him.

··

MORAL OF THE STORY
Fatalistic envy brings out the worst in you.

··

J

is for
JESSA THE
JADED JELLY BEAN

The crowded, competitive world of jelly beans was really getting to Jessa the Jaded Jelly Bean.

Why were all the other beans so obsessed with outdoing each other?

Why did there have to be feuding cliques and incessant gossiping?

Also, did it really matter what flavour you were?

As a Juicy Pear flavour with a sewage-green coating, Jessa was well aware that she was considered one of the mediocre jelly beans who would never reach the pleasing popularity of the pink Bubblegum jelly beans, or be elevated to the yummy ranks of the Toasted Marshmallow jelly beans. Meanwhile, the Pomegranate and Acai Berry jelly beans refused to allow her into their Superfruit Sorority because of her lack of antioxidants.

"I didn't ask to be born as a Juicy Pear flavour. Why must this be the only thing people judge me by?" she asked fellow outcasts Cinnamon and Liquorice jelly beans. They sighed, full of ennui, and simply did not bother to answer such futile rhetorical questions.

Jessa decided that she had to do something to improve the situation of marginalised beans like herself. During the next monthly town hall meeting, she made her case.

"I strongly believe that every bean is equal. Beans like me deserve to be at the top of the jar every once in a while!" she said passionately.

The Superfruit jelly beans sniggered at such unfeasible idealism. The Bubblegum jelly beans jumped about in protest at the audacity of such an idea. However, Toasted Marshmallow jelly bean smiled gently at Jessa and told her to come stand next to him.

"Hear ye, hear ye, beans of the jar! We have a sister jelly bean here who is a true visionary. She spoke the words that have been resting heavily in my heart for a while," he said.

"In order for beans like Jessa to move up the jar as she so rightly deserves, I would like you to welcome new jelly beans to our midst so that we can create more meritocratic opportunities for all jelly beans to move up the jar. Ladies and gentlemen, please welcome our candy comrades from the thrilling Gothic range to our jar: Vomit, Earthworm and Booger!"

All the beans, including Jessa, gasped in horror. But there was nothing they could do. It was just going to get more cut-throat from now onwards.

MORAL OF THE STORY
Idealism usually ends up being a
double-edged sword in reality.

K

is for

KIP THE
KLUTZY KINGFISHER

Kip the Klutzy Kingfisher once got into a fight with a seagull over a fish. He lost part of his left wing and was unable to fly. His wife, Kate, had to take over the hunting while he was left to tend to their five babies. It was hard on Kip — he used to be respected as one of the top fishers in the forest, but now, he was a harried domestic nest-husband who tended to squawking babies all day long.

Kip missed hanging out with the boys, but it was impossible to catch up with them since they mostly socialised while cruising above the tree canopies, or scoping out river spots with plenty of fish.

He felt useless. He felt bored. He felt like he didn't know who he was any more.

Every night, Kip would have either of these dreams: flying amongst fluffy white clouds with the wind in his feathers or pecking the eyeballs out from the seagull who ruined his life. Both dreams made him cry when he woke up.

Poor Kate — she too was getting dragged down by Kip's despair and the burden of finding enough food for the whole family. Once their babies flew the nest, she told Kip that she needed to spread her wings as well so that she could find herself again.

Poor Kip was all alone. He now had to rely on the charity of his old friends who would send over insects or leftover fish scraps so that he would not starve to death.

With such a miserable existence, Kip began belting out haunting melodies in minor keys, and often, his weepy crooning would make nearby animals weep.

One day, a passing ornithologist heard him singing and was intrigued by such uncharacteristic birdsong coming out from a kingfisher. He took Kip back to his climate-controlled laboratory where Kip now gets a thick slab of Norwegian wild salmon every day and lives with six gorgeous Buff-Breasted Kingfishers.

MORAL OF THE STORY
When you're already at your lowest point,
things can only get better.

L

is for
LUCY THE
LIVELY LEEK

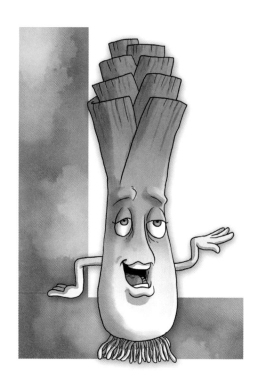

Lucy the Lively Leek was always talking, and talking, and talking. As such, the other vegetables could not stand her.

Oliver the Obnoxious Onion would often tell her that she was a "a pale floozy with green shoots for brains".

Geraldine the Grating Garlic, would never fail to point out Lucy's stinky breath every time the chatty leek opened her mouth.

Brian the Bored Broccoli would unfailingly roll his eyes every time Lucy looked like she was about to say something.

But Lucy couldn't help it. She really just loved chatter. Her monologues were a way of making sense of life and reaching out to the rest of the vegetable community.

However, as Lucy continued to get berated or ignored, she gradually began to realise that she had to quieten down so as to become more palatable to the other vegetables. Some days, she would not even say anything at all.

All that changed one day when a bag of potatoes was introduced to the vegetable drawer. These playful, down-to-earth spuds were always cracking jokes and giggling amongst themselves. When the other vegetables would try to shush them, they would just break out into louder guffaws.

They also loved conversing about everything under the sun — from soil types to politics to philosophy. Lucy

enjoyed bantering with them so much that she decided
to move into the potato bag where finally, she felt like
she belonged.

It also helped that with their multiple eyes, the potatoes
always looked like they were interested in what she had
to say.

MORAL OF THE STORY
Having the right friends makes all the difference.

M
is for
MING THE
MOROSE MANDARIN

Ming sighed as he looked at the towering pile of files on his office desk.

These documents contained confidential information on undesirable behaviour committed by compromised artists. He had to write formal reports on all these cases by the end of the week.

Whatever had possessed him to accept this research officer posting to the Ministry of Moral Conduct? Ah yes, his parents had told him it was the "respectable" thing to do.

What Ming really wanted to do was dance. Ever since he had watched a ballet production of *The Nutcracker* as a child, he knew that prancing around on stage would bring him the greatest of joys.

However, Ming was never able to become a professional dancer despite learning ballet for over a decade. He was always rejected at auditions for having the "wrong body type".

"It was a blessing in disguise," his friends would comfort him of his failed dance career. "Now, you have a cushy job while the government is shutting down dance schools for being too subversive."

But it was hard for Ming the Morose Mandarin to feel gratitude when the mind-numbing routine of generating behavioural reports was draining his zest for life. It also didn't help that the data he dealt with were often about other fruits who seemed to lead way more exciting lives than him.

They would probably disappear after Ming submitted the reports, but at least they would have lived passionately during their brief period of existence.

Ming sighed again as he flipped open the file from the top of the pile. This time, the information was on Barry the Ballerino Banana. Ming admired CCTV photos showing Barry gracefully pirouetting in the studio.

Suddenly, a brilliant idea dawned on him. What if he transferred to the fieldwork department and specifically asked to investigate dance companies by posing as a freelance dancer?

He had the right qualifications and experience, and more importantly, he actually knew how to dance with a Grade 8 Certificate in Ballet, so he would blend right in.

Also, since there were already a few spies in prominent positions within these dance companies, it would be guaranteed that he would get through the auditions for a change.

Ming drafted out his Request for Transfer e-mail to his boss and Human Resources. He was pretty sure they would agree to his proposal because the Ballet Resistance was growing stronger by the day. There needed to be someone who would keep tabs on the dancing dissidents from the ground level.

It would be the best of both worlds — Ming would feed his artistic soul by being a professional dancer while still being paid a generous civil servant salary.

<hr>

MORAL OF THE STORY
If your job sucks, be resourceful
about finding ways to have it suck less.

<hr>

N

is for

NELLY THE
NICE NECKLACE

These days, it was hard for Nelly to play nice. She was getting increasingly annoyed at the rest of the jewellery in the Box. They never let her forget that she was better suited to being on the 1930s Disney version of Snow White as opposed to Owner, who was a fashionable corporate banker.

"Oh Nelly! Whatever should we do with you? Your sterling silver chain makes you too expensive to be costume jewellery, but your polka-dot plastic ribbon is so, how should I put it, *quaint*," said Delilah the Diva Diamond Choker with an airy chuckle.

Boris the Boorish Bvlgari Bracelet sniffed. "You know, if you were branded, say perchance you originated from the House of Chanel, perhaps you could have passed off as kitsch high fashion which is all the rage this Spring Season. But dearie me, the only label on you says 'Made in China'," he scoffed with a stiff upper lip.

The rest of the jewellery tittered.

"Oh, shut up!" Nelly retorted. "You and Delilah and everyone else here were made in China as well."

Everyone gasped. Did Nelly, sweet Nelly, who couldn't even be worn on Owner's neck without trembling, just show some attitude?

In fact, now that she wasn't putting on her usual demure, slightly forlorn smile, she actually looked rather menacing, like a nasty necklace with chicken pox.

Boris, who was much bulkier than Nelly, rolled right up to her and gave a menacing stare. "You better know your place here in the Box. And never forget that your face is all plastic."

Delilah made it a point to blind Nelly with her bling so that her eyes would water.

"Oh Nelly, dear Nelly. You don't know what you're in for now," Delilah remarked with a flick of her velvet ribbon.

Just as Boris and Diva were about to intimidate Nelly further, the Box opened.

Owner was showing her five-year-old daughter her jewellery. The little girl oohed and aahed at the shimmery splendour of Diva's diamonds, but it was Nelly that she picked up from the Box.

"Mummy, can I have this necklace? It's so pretty!" she cooed.

"Of course, you can, sweetie. This is one of my favourite necklaces. I wore it when I was a little girl like you and it always made me feel like a princess! Take good care of it, okay?" Owner said as she cuddled her daughter.

"Yes, Mummy, I will! Thank you!"

The little girl was jumping up and down with unadulterated joy as the Owner carefully hooked Nelly around her daughter's neck.

As the Box was shut, faint sighs of envy could be heard from the rest of the jewellery who hadn't been out in a very, very long time.

MORAL OF THE STORY
Humble beginnings do not necessarily
mean humble endings.

O

is for

OLIVIA THE
OVERACHIEVING OCTOPUS

Olivia the Overachieving Octopus had just laid 100,000 eggs in her lair.

Now, she was writing a to-do list to prepare for the arrival of her offspring. After using her ink to write out a list of 64 tasks to do (her target was always to do eight things with each of her eight arms each day), she hailed a ride from Sammy the Speedy Sailfish to the Golden Palace, her workplace of ten years where she served as the personal assistant to King Neptune.

This was a job that she loved — the pace was challenging and she loved meeting such a diverse range of creatures from the oceanic kingdom. Most importantly, her high-profile position had inspired many other female sea creatures to consider empowering careers as well. Last year, she was the first female sea creature to receive the Marine Gold Service award for her outstanding work performance.

When Olivia arrived at the palace, she was surprised to observe King Neptune being particularly quiet and antsy. Usually, in the mornings, he would be regaling the royal court with dramatic accounts of defeating assorted sea monsters in his youth.

In an attempt to cheer him up, Olivia presented him with his favourite home-made seaweed pie that she'd baked the night before, but even that didn't seem to warm him up.

Finally, after much swishing up and down his throne, King Neptune told Olivia that he had to let her go.

"You know my daughter … she is getting so restless and keeps going up on land to flirt with those two-legged men. I have no choice but to keep a closer eye on her and I thought I'd give her something to do while she's kept at the palace. I was thinking that being my PA would be an easy enough job for her..." King Neptune trailed off when he saw Olivia's face darken. Even though he was immortal, octopus ink was never fun to scrub off.

Olivia took a few seconds to collect herself before responding.

"Of course, Your Majesty, I understand. In any case, I do need the time to prepare for the babies. They're hatching any day from now. The princess is such a bright young mermaid, I'm sure she will learn a lot from this job."

A relieved King Neptune proceeded to present a generous compensation package to Olivia the Overachieving Octopus: a whole crate of clams she could feast on and ten gold coins from his treasury. But this did not make Olivia feel any better. She burst into tears the minute she left the Golden Palace.

Whatever was she going to do with her life now? All the other jobs for women in the ocean were all beneath her. She also had no intention of just taking care of her young ones either — her friends turned so boring and frumpy after they became full-time baby-slaves.

Olivia was so distracted by her job loss that she failed to see a fishing net in front of her. The fishermen were absolutely delighted at such a great catch and Olivia was served as fresh *tako* sashimi that very same evening to a group of Japanese businessmen.

··

MORAL OF THE STORY
Never let work determine your sense of worth.

··

P
is for
PAUL THE
PSYCHIC PILLOW

Everywhere that Polly went, her pillow was sure to go. Her attachment to this particular pillow was so deep that she'd even given him a name: Paul.

Paul had been given to Polly when she was four and had to sleep in her first grown-up bed. They'd been inseparable ever since. She brought him to school, to the movies, and sometimes even on dates!

Nobody thought of this as anything more than an adorably quirky attachment. However, no one knew that Paul was actually a magic pillow, and Polly could communicate silently with him just by laying her head on him.

Paul was also able to suss other people out just by getting them to place their heads on him. This had become the default way for Polly to screen her boyfriends.

One day, Polly met David, who seemed like the perfect guy. He was good-looking but not vain, intelligent but not condescending, kind but not a pushover. They instantly connected and could talk for hours. She knew that she was falling in love with him, but also wanted Paul the Psychic Pillow to scan him first.

However, David refused to lie on Polly's pillow for hygiene reasons.

Polly had to resort to drugging David via a romantic home-made dinner at home. After tucking Paul under an unconscious David's head, she too lay down on Paul, next to David.

"So, Paul, what do you think? Is he the man I should marry?"

Polly was anxious for a confirmation because David had hinted that he was looking around for an engagement ring.

There was a long pause. Finally, Paul replied, "OK here's the good news: this guy here really loves you now, but..."

"But? There's a 'but'? Tell me what this 'but' is about," Polly silently screamed at Paul.

"Okay, okay... With this guy, this is probably your last shot at true love. But it won't last long. Ten years from now, David will cheat on you with his secretary and your son will run away from home when he is 18. The fact is, once you guys have a kid, you'll become this terrifying and over-possessive matriarch who never knows when to let go."

Polly flung Paul the Psychic Pillow across the room and took a few deep breaths to collect herself. When she finally pulled herself together after a few minutes, she grabbed a pair of scissors and started ripping her once-beloved pillow apart. When David woke up from his nap, he found Polly filling up a trash bag with Paul's shredded remains.

"Honey, I'm so glad you're getting rid of that baby pillow of yours. It was a dust hazard," David said.

"Hey sweetie?" Polly tried to keep her tone casual. "Shall we not have kids when we get married?"

MORAL OF THE STORY
Don't succumb to fate — chart your own destiny.

Q

is for

QUEENIE THE
QUIET QUILT

Queenie the Quiet Quilt was usually the silent observer when it came to bed bickering. Benjamin the Boisterous Bolster would hit Patsy the Petty Pillow and tell her she was infested by cooties, while Patsy would smother Benjamin and declare him a stinky drool sponge. Then they'd look over at Queenie and ask, "What are you looking at?" accusingly.

Queenie ignored them most of the time, and longed for the good old days when her bedmates were cleaner and politer. She actually did wonder why she was still here when all her bedfellow peers were long gone.

One day, Patsy and Benjamin were sent for sunning, while Queenie and the rest of the bed linen were sent for a soapy spin in the washing machine. This only meant one thing: a visitor was coming. Queenie dreaded that — she didn't like to be in contact with strangers.

However, when the visitor, an old lady in her seventies, arrived, she obviously seemed to recognise Queenie, because she grabbed the quilt tightly with both hands.

"Grandma, why are you hugging the dirty blanket?" a young girl asked the old lady.

"I'll tell you later during bedtime, dear," the old lady replied as she sniffed Queenie and smiled.

Later, when there was no one in the guest room, Patsy the Petty Pillow threw a fit because she didn't want any stray hairs landing on her, while Benjamin the Boisterous Bolster was rolling around dramatically, bemoaning that old people's drool was gross. Throughout the commotion, Queenie remained silent and deep in thought. While she'd initially felt manhandled by this old lady, something about her smell and her voice felt familiar.

That night, the old lady invited the little girl up on bed with her as she spread Queenie across both their bodies.

"This blanket here is called a quilt," the old lady told the little girl. "It was a plain white blanket at first, but later, I started adding square patches to it so I wouldn't forget certain moments in my life.

"See here? I started out with this pink patch because that was the colour of my wedding dress. I later added this patch with sunflowers, because these were the first flowers I planted in my very first home with Grandpa. When I was pregnant with your mummy, I included a blue patch, because I thought she was going to be a boy. Later, I added this rainbow patch here, to remind us of better days ahead during the time your grandpa lost his job ..."

As the old lady rattled on, Queenie gradually realised that this lady was her creator, and felt something she hadn't felt in a long time: it was a feeling of being at home.

" ... and when your mummy turned seven, I let her have this quilt, which she still keeps up till today. Will you promise Grandma you'll help take care of this quilt too?"

The little girl nodded and yawned.

"Grandma, can you put me to bed?"

After the old lady and the little girl left the guestroom, Queenie pranced up and down the bed.

"I remember! I remember now!" she cried joyously. Patsy and Benjamin jumped up in surprise.

"I told you Queenie wasn't mute!" Benjamin told Patsy.

"Well, how was I supposed to know? This is the first time I'm hearing her voice," Patsy snapped back.

The old lady returned to the room later and spent a long time tracing her fingers gently over each patch on Queenie till she fell asleep.

The next morning, the family found the old lady in bed, not breathing but with a peaceful facial expression. She was still warm because the quilt had been draped over her.

MORAL OF THE STORY
Don't be so quick to throw old keepsakes away.

R
is for
RANDY THE
RESENTFUL REINDEER

Randy was supposed to have been at the front all along, leading the sleigh of reindeer. He was taller, had shinier antlers and had a much better sense of direction than his loser baby brother Rudolph. Santa was an idiot.

It all started in 1949 at the peak of Cold War tensions. The PR Elf was telling Santa that his ratings were down and that he needed to do something to create a more "accessible" image.

His advice? Be less WASP Father Christmas and more "Gandhi in a winter wardrobe". Embody this embracing love for mankind.

As such, Santa decided that the ugliest, most slobbery reindeer would lead the pack that Christmas, to show how inclusive and benevolent he was. Rudolph, with his perpetually scruffy fur, cracked right antler and sinus issues, was picked.

At first, Randy didn't mind the time off — it really was a backbreaking delivery round every Christmas. But when Rudolph actually started getting famous with that stupid Christmas song, that's when Randy really got pissed.

The worst part was that all the other reindeer were also mentioned in the Christmas song — everyone except him, the original leader! And, of course, because the *Rudolph the Red-Nosed Reindeer* single sold 25 million copies around the world and was now a Christmas carol staple, Rudolph's position as lead reindeer became permanent.

It had been this way for over 60 years and Randy the Resentful Reindeer had had enough of this ridiculous arrangement. It was just so unfair. Rudolph even married the prettiest reindeer in the North Pole, Vixen, who bore more snot-faced reindeers that made Randy grimace every time they grazed near him.

Randy's buddies, Dasher and Comet, felt sorry for him — he'd been the top reindeer for Santa for a long time and he was an excellent navigator. They'd often complain to Randy about how on top of all the presents, they also had to carry cartons of tissue paper for Rudolph's drippy red nose, and how even with GPS these days, Rudolph would still lose his way. But Dasher and Comet never showed any inkling of contempt in front of Santa, because they didn't want to rock the sleigh.

One day, Randy the Resentful Reindeer could no longer bear this injustice and barged into Santa's office. "Look, old man, don't you think it's about time I'm lead reindeer again? You told me this Rudolph thing was meant to be a temporary arrangement," Randy growled.

Santa sighed. It got tiring when minions acted up.

"You're already doing such a good job teaching survival skills to the young reindeer in the North Pole, Randy. Besides, PR Elf says that I really can't change my sleigh reindeer line-up because of that Christmas song. I'm so sorry, Randy," Santa explained and proceeded to offer him a candy cane.

Just at that moment, Rudolph stomped into the office and threw his resignation letter down on Santa's table.

"Look here, old man, I QUIT. I'm absolutely *exhausted* after six decades of Christmas sleigh-pulling. My sinuses aren't getting any better with all that exposure to high-altitude chill and I want to spend more time with my kids. You promised me I could retire 10 years ago, you slave-driver!"

The PR Elf scuttled into Santa's office to see what all the commotion was about. Upon hearing Randy's and Rudolph's respective grouses, he came up with a win-win solution: Rudolph would retire and Randy would go through reconstructive surgery to get a red nose, a cracked right antler and scruffy fur to pass off as Rudolph with more muscles. "We'll just say Rudolph is now on a whole foods diet and works out with a personal trainer," the PR Elf said.

Randy, who was now known as Rudolph, was happy to be back in the game — at least for the first three years. But over time, he began to regret sacrificing his good looks for ambition. And so, he became a resentful reindeer again — but this time, one with a shiny red nose.

....

MORAL OF THE STORY
Be careful what you wish for.

....

S

is for
SHEILA THE
SLEEPY SALMON

"Oi, Sheila, wake up!"

Sheila the Sleepy Salmon slowly opened her eyes to see the entire school looking at her disapprovingly. Some of them were even wagging their fins at her. She had fallen asleep — again — while they were crossing the ocean, and had been trailing behind until the Head Salmon slapped her awake.

Sheila suppressed a yawn as the Head Salmon launched into one of those serious talks again... perilous journey blah blah blah... need to be a more proactive team player blah blah blah... she'd heard it all before. It's not as if she deliberately wanted to create trouble.

Sometimes, Sheila wondered how she'd ended up as an Atlantic Salmon, especially when she didn't have an aggressive bone in her. But being a salmon always required her to swim, swim, swim, hunt, hunt, hunt, fight, fight, fight. If left to her own devices, she'd much rather be chatting with the clams or admiring colourful coral.

This meaningless flurry of activity was taking its toll on Sheila, and she grabbed every opportunity to get some shut-eye. With sleep came dreams. With dreams came the possibilities of one day living a slower, more deliberate way of life.

"We're the King of Fish, you cannot just go around falling asleep like that. Sheila? Sheila! Are you listening to me?" Head Salmon slapped her again with his fin.

Before Sheila could nod, a colony of sea lions pounced on the school of salmon. Sheila managed to duck to a corner among some rocks to hide, an instinctive response to all the times she would try to hide from Head Salmon's wrath. When the sea lions left with full bellies, Sheila looked around the other rocks and found a few of the younger salmon who had also survived the attack.

The poor young fish were absolutely traumatised by the brutal massacre and were sobbing hysterically. Sheila gathered them together and led them through some deep gill-breathing exercises to help them calm down. Once they were able to swim in a more stable manner, she led them to a sunken ship where they could seek shelter for the night. There, she sang them sweet lullabies till the young salmons' fins stopped twitching.

Sleep was no longer a form of escapism, it was now a matter of survival. Only rest would give them the strength to press through for rest of their journey.

MORAL OF THE STORY
In the hustle and bustle of life,
we all could do with more rest.

T

is for
TIMMY THE
TENACIOUS TEABAG

Morale was low in the snacks pantry — after all, if you weren't going to be eaten, you were going to get scorched in boiling water. The teabags and instant coffee sachets would often huddle together in the darkest corner of the pantry, bemoaning about their impending torturous deaths.

Timmy the Tenacious Teabag, however, refused to get looped into their circle of despair. He plotted his escape. You see, the potato-chip packets had told him how a few of their predecessors had managed to hitch a ride from a group of revolutionary rats who sympathised with the snacks' wretched fates. They managed to set up a meeting between Timmy and the revolutionary rat leader.

"Teabags seldom survive for more than a day in the outside world," the revolutionary rat leader warned. "Why do you long for your freedom so much?"

"Dear Sir Rat, I miss the mountains. I miss the smell of fresh dew in the morning. Most of all, I miss being a plant again, spreading my leaves out in the sunlight and truly connecting with nature. I really need to go back to the tea plantation to restore my soul," Timmy replied earnestly.

The revolutionary rat leader nodded his head approvingly, and said, "It is a wonderful dream to aspire towards, Timmy. Very well, two of my men will help you to get out tonight."

That night, Timmy was whisked away from the snacks pantry and brought to the revolutionary rats' hideout in the storeroom. From there, Timmy had expected to meet the revolutionary rat leader to receive more instructions on how he was going to make his way to the tea plantation. But instead, he saw a horde of rats gathered around a broken teacup filled with steaming hot water.

Oh no, he had been duped! The rats had wanted to drink him and had only pretended to offer him an escape plan!

Maybe they'd devoured the packets of potato chips who had supposedly escaped too!

The revolutionary rat leader came out in a black formal robe as Timmy was being carried towards the teacup by two muscular rats.

"Thank you," said the leader, as he bowed respectfully to Timmy.

"How could you do this? You tricked me, you evil rat!" Timmy yelled.

The rat shook his head.

"We need you, Timmy. You'll provide us with the energy and focus to plan our attacks tonight, and you'll also give us the antioxidants for strength to kill those cat terrorists who have been attacking us for far too long. Don't take it as a betrayal, I'd hate for you to see it like that. From now on, you will be considered a heroic martyr in the much-needed liberation of repressed rodents."

Before Timmy could say "rubbish", he was thrown into the teacup with hot water. The rats clapped and cheered.

MORAL OF THE STORY
You can never go back to your past again.

U

is for

UMBERTO THE
UPBEAT UMBRELLA

What goes up when the rain comes down?

An umbrella, of course! And how glad Umberto was to be one!

After all, he was fulfilling an essential societal role — shading people from raindrops and keeping them dry. He loved having big fat raindrops trickle down his face, being shaken dry like a wet dog and getting a nice crispy texture after being sunned. It was a simple existence with simple joys, but one which he wholeheartedly found meaningful.

Every time it rained, Umberto was taken out of the bag and opened up towards the sky, where he would make it a point to greet Lady Rain respectfully. She was, after all, pretty much the basis of his existence. However, Lady Rain would either ignore him or pass a snarky remark about his rusty metal frame.

One day, Lady Rain was in a particularly foul mood and threw a thunderstorm.

"Good morning, Lady Rain. I see that you're really in your element today," Umberto remarked.

Lady Rain rumbled with rage.

"YOU THINK YOU'RE REALLY SOMETHING, AREN'T YOU? ALWAYS SMILING EVEN THOUGH I'VE MADE THE SKIES CRY. WHO DO YOU THINK YOU ARE?" Lady Rain howled.

"Oh, pardon me, ma'am. I never meant to be rude or anything. I just really enjoy my job, which is helping people move around on a rainy day."

"AND MAKING PEOPLE FORGET MY EXISTENCE... OF THE POWER I HAVE OVER THEM? YOU UMBRELLAS ARE

REALLY SOMETHING!" Lady Rain howled. She proceeded to hurl a huge gust of wind so strong that Umberto ended up getting flipped up.

"THERE, I'VE MADE YOU EVEN MORE UPBEAT AND USELESS."

As a final touch, Lady Rain let out a flash of lightning that hit Umberto's metal tip and gave his Holder a rude electrical shock. Umberto fell to the ground, and helplessly watched the chaos that ensued as the police and an ambulance came to help his unconscious Holder.

"Lady Rain, why did you do this? I've been nothing but polite to you all these years. And my poor Holder — she never spews vulgarities at you when you come down, unlike most other human beings, and this is how you treat her? You are horrid!"

More lightning and thunder ensued, which angered Umberto even more. He was about to say more harsh words to Lady Rain, when he realised that she was actually crying.

"NO ONE CARES ABOUT ME ANYMORE. BOO HOO HOOOOOOOO ..."

Umberto then realised that Lady Rain was feeling unappreciated and probably was not aware of her importance in the environment. Fortunately, his previous Holder had been a geography teacher, so he had picked up some things along the way.

"Oh Lady Rain, that is far from true. Even though you are worshipped by only a few surviving tribes today, your role in keeping all of us alive here remains! You're always in the news every day, and many scientists around the world study you in great detail. You matter to us, much more than you will ever realise," Umberto explained gently to her.

After such nurturing reassurance, Lady Rain calmed down to a drizzle.

"Thank you for telling me this, Umberto. I've never thought about my existence this way but you're right! You are not only upbeat, but understanding as well," she said with a serene smile.

The clouds cleared and the sun came out. Someone picked Umberto up from the ground, flipped him back to his original shape, and shook him dry.

Umberto eagerly awaited Lady Rain's next visit.

MORAL OF THE STORY
Being chirpy is good, but you should also be sensitive to other people's problems.

V

is for
VALERIE THE
VICIOUS VESPA

Jason and Valerie made quite a pair. Everyone said they looked so cute together.

When he rode her, they exuded carefree bohemian vibes. To Valerie, they were a match made in heaven.

One day, Jason met Jane at an outdoor music festival. Jason offered Jane a lift home. Valerie did not appreciate the extra passenger, and deliberately stalled a few times at the traffic lights to express her displeasure.

This was the first time Valerie heard Jason swearing at her (softly, but still).

As time went by, Jane the pillion rider became a regular fixture, and no amount of stalling on Valerie's part seemed to discourage that. In fact, it just meant more trips back to the workshop with grubby and smelly mechanics, much to Valerie's dismay.

Something more drastic had to be done. Valerie consulted Harry the Hunky Harley, who was sometimes parked next to her at Jason's car park. Harry's owner often went stunt-riding, so Harry was familiar with manoeuvring angles and speeds that would create certain outcomes.

Meanwhile, Jason and Jane continued getting very serious, and one night, Jason proposed to Jane with a whimsical hemp ring (she accepted, that bitch).

When this happened, Valerie had no choice but to execute a spectacular wheelie, where she lifted her front wheel off the ground so that she could fling Jane to the road.

Jane's arms and legs were bloody, and the baby-pink helmet Jason bought for her had cracked. While waiting for the ambulance to come, Jason was holding on to an unconscious Jane and bawling. Valerie suddenly realised how big his nostrils were and she began to wonder why she had bothered to gone through so much trouble for this wimpy human.

Meanwhile, as Jason accompanied Jane into the ambulance, he turned back to look at the accident scene and stared at Valerie suspiciously.

Fortunately, Jane recovered from her minor head concussion and superficial wounds within a few weeks and started planning for their wedding. Her parents gave Jason an ultimatum: drive a proper car, or they were not going to pay for the wedding ceremony by the beach with a shoegaze band as entertainment.

Jason proceeded to buy a vintage yellow Volkswagen Beetle. He could have sold Valerie off easily because she was a lovingly-restored classic 1978 Vespa 100 Sport model. But in the end, he decided to scrap Valerie once and for all.

....

MORAL OF THE STORY
The more psycho one gets, the more likely the psychotic scheming will backfire.

....

W

is for
WALTER THE
WISTFUL WOMBAT

More than anything else in the world, Walter the Wistful Wombat wanted to fly. However, in reality, he would spend his waking hours just burrowing about in the ground. At least his cousins, the koalas, could climb and get some semblance of elevation. Walter had often begged them to carry him up a eucalyptus tree so he would get a sense of being above the ground, but they just laughed at the idea and told him he was too fat to be carried up.

Whatever was Walter to do? Whining got him nowhere; neither did wishing on shooting stars for a pair of wings. As the likelihood of him flying across the sky diminished, so too did his appetite and size as he found nothing to look forward to in life.

Walter's little brother, Wilfred the Wacky Wombat, felt sorry that Walter was so forlorn. He began devising a brilliant plan to make his brother's dream of flight come true.

One day, while Walter was having an afternoon nap, Wilfred snuck a little handmade parachute package into his pouch. From there, four koalas brought him to the top of the tallest tree in the forest (now that he had lost some weight, the koalas were agreeable to giving him that ride).

Once Walter was brought to the top, the koalas woke him up and told him to enjoy the view of the mountains. Then, they told him to jump and pull the string tucked into his parachute pouch. Walter did just that and floated down, crying with happiness.

Walter was on cloud nine for the next few days and couldn't stop talking about how transformative and uplifting that experience had been. He gave Wilfred a snuggly hug and told him he was the best brother in the world.

However, after a week, Walter became bored and aimless again. He pestered Wilfred to make him automated wings so that he could fly around the forest on his own and he badgered the koalas to ask the eagles if they could give him a lift up to the mountaintop.

Everyone grew really annoyed by Walter's indulgent demands and the koala cousins arranged for Katy the Kooky Kangaroo to plop him into her pouch and bring him to a forest far, far away so they could finally get some peace and quiet.

MORAL OF THE STORY
Appreciate what you have or you'll
continue hankering for more.

X

is for

XAVIER THE
XENIAL X-RAY MACHINE

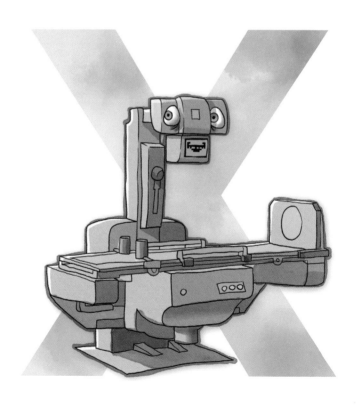

Xavier saw people for who they were on the inside, and because of that, many patients feared him at the hospital.

Despite, or perhaps because of this, Xavier loved everyone he met. Humans came in all shapes and sizes, and yet, when he shone his beam on them, they were fundamentally similar — trembling, vulnerable beings who were seriously considering their mortality when they came to him. If it weren't for the side effects of the radiation, Xavier would have loved to spend more time comforting each patient with his warm aura.

However, Mr Tan, was different. He ambled into the radiology room one day and started talking to Xavier. This was unusual. Most patients just wanted to get the whole thing over with and hardly ever glanced at the X-ray machine.

"You may think there's something wrong with me after you do your 'bling-bling'. But here's a secret: this is the best thing that has ever happened to me. Suddenly, I see everything for what it is."

Xavier scanned Mr Tan's skull and was not surprised to detect a large white mass in the right frontal lobe of his brain. Based on his experience, this was probably a Stage 3 or Stage 4 malignant tumour. What a pity.

"Xavier? You call yourself Xavier, don't you? What an apt name. You have saved many people with the work you do. Thank you."

Xavier switched himself off in shock. What kind of sorcery was this?

The radiologist came in hurriedly, apologising.

"Mr Tan, I'm sorry, this X-ray machine is cranky today, but we've already got what we needed. The neurologist will go over the scans with you later."

Mr Tan winked at Xavier as he walked out.

All this while, Xavier had been content helping patients silently from the sidelines. Having his existence so kindly acknowledged for the first time in his life made him yearn for yet another interaction with Mr Tan.

It was a few months later when Mr Tan showed up in the radiology room again, this time in a wheelchair. Xavier whirred excitedly as a form of greeting.

"I'm glad to see you too," said Mr Tan as he smiled at the X-ray machine.

"So Xavier," continued Mr Tan, "I have a favour. I know that my tumour has grown. The doctors and my family are going to see your scans and they are going to make me go through a major operation to remove it."

"But I don't want to. These past few months of being immersed in this expanded form of existence has been wonderful. I've lived long enough: my wife's gone, my children have all grown up, and I'm content just to spend my last days like this. Do you think you can you do something about it?"

Xavier could and he did. He did not completely remove the growth from the film for that would be too suspicious. Instead, he shrunk it down and smoothened its edges enough for the doctor to think the tumour wasn't too serious.

The radiologist entered the room looking frustrated again.

"Sorry this took a while, Mr Tan. I don't know why this X-ray machine is working so slowly today. The next time you come, we'll be using a brand-new machine, not this temperamental old one."

As Mr Tan was wheeled out of the room, he raised his right hand to give a grateful 'thank you' salute to Xavier. In return, Xavier emitted the tiniest flick of light as he bade his friend a fond farewell.

MORAL OF THE STORY
It's possible to find true friends late in life, and usually in the unlikeliest of circumstances.

Y

is for
YOLANDA THE
YOUNG-AT-HEART YACHT

Everyone knew Yolanda at the marina club. She was the pioneer of boat parties, and in the 1990s, every tycoon and magnate in this region was well-acquainted with her. Even before "YOLO" became a popular acronym amongst the millennials, the socialites back in the day would casually brag to each other about "Yolo-ing" i.e. getting exclusively invited to party on Yolanda by the Captain.

Over the years, however, as the marina club membership soared and more private yachts came to berth, "Yolo-ing" didn't quite hold so much appeal. In fact, it had become the unofficial "old fogey's boat" where the Captain was more likely to organise offshore fishing trips these days.

This greatly distressed Yolanda the Young-at-Heart Yacht. She wanted beautiful people, Ibiza lounge music and champagne fountains, not pot-bellied uncles chugging Tiger Beer and hauling up spluttering, gouged fish that left bloody puddles on her sparkly deck.

"Babe, you've got to help me here. The Captain has like, totally let himself go these past few years, and I. Just. Cannot," Yolanda confided to Petrice the Patient Powerboat.

"Yolo, sweetie, I feel for you, I really do. But you've got to remember you're not a spring chicken yourself anymore, you know? The Captain got you back what — 20, 25 years ago? You should be so glad he still bothers to send you for servicing and spray-painting every year. Many boats your age would have been canned by now. You've just got to accept that you're in the sunset stage of life right now," Petrice explained to her gently.

Yolanda sulked. She didn't feel old, and she definitely felt that she had a good few years of partying left. As she stewed angrily in her berth, a brochure flew in and landed on one of her sun beds.

SUPER YACHT SHOW

*An Exclusive Gathering
to Celebrate Luxury Yachts
Past, Present and Future*

****

"Thank you, Captain, for loaning us Yolanda. I don't know why, but I suddenly kept noticing how classically stylish she was last week while we were setting up for the show near the berths. And then I realised, she would be perfect as the heritage centrepiece at the concourse. In fact, we're holding our VIP event launch with her later tonight — she is going to be a star!" said an excitable man decked in a fitted white suit and Armani sunglasses.

The Captain shrugged and thought nothing much of it. He was more into golf than fishing these days.

Meanwhile, Yolanda was enjoying the attention that she was receiving now that she had been prominently placed on an elevated red carpet platform. A famous German DJ with dreadlocks and multiple piercings was on her deck testing out the sound system while handsome butlers were setting up a champagne fountain and bringing in trays of assorted caviar canapes.

"Now, this is how you enjoy a sunset," Yolanda thought to herself as she took in the rich red-orange hued sky.

MORAL OF THE STORY
We can't stop growing old. But it doesn't mean we can't be fabulous about it.

Z

is for

ZECHARIAH THE ZEALOUS ZEBRA

The zoo animals were planning a mass breakout, but it had been a struggle ironing out the details while trying to hide this massive operation from Zechariah the Zealous Zebra.

If Zechariah got as much as a whiff of their escape plans, they knew he would not hesitate to out them to the zookeepers.

However, one night, Zechariah paid a surprise visit to the ostrich compound and discovered that the holes he thought contained their eggs were actually portals to a complex network of escape tunnels. The plan was this: the smaller animals would travel through these tunnels to get out of the zoo. Once they had escaped outside, these animals would open the zoo's main gates to let everybody else out.

"To think I'd put in all this effort to prepare lovely baby hampers for the upcoming hatchings, you awful ostriches. In fact, all of you are just plain awful! How could you ever think of pulling off something like this?" Zechariah screeched when he confronted his zoo-mates.

"Our zookeepers would be heartbroken if you all just up and left like that. We're a family!" He slammed his front hoof against a feeding trough in anger.

Geraldine the Gentle Giraffe spoke up. "It's not as black and white as this, Zechariah. Most of our zookeepers are nice, but we're wildlife — we're meant to be in our natural habitats like forests, jungles and oceans. Being kept in enclosures and cages has had terrible mental and physical side effects on many of us and we have had enough. Just last month, Billy the Baboon started throwing himself repeatedly against the primates glass enclosure because he saw hallucinations of his late mother. Just like that, he was put to sleep the next day. The minute any one of us receives a visitor complaint or is deemed not a money maker, the zoo has no qualms about getting rid of us."

Zechariah shook his head vehemently. "Zoos protect us. We're all endangered species. We were all brought here for good reason; to heal the fractured state of the animal kingdom. Over here, we're fed well, we're given space to run around and we're given medicine when we're sick. Come on Geraldine, you just gave birth to George last year with the help from the best vets in the world. If you were still living in the plains, which are mostly deforested these days by the way, the lions would have eaten you and George up in an instant. You have to look at the bigger picture here, animal brethren. I hope you understand but I have no choice but to sound off the emergency alarm system right now ..."

WHOOSH! ROAR! RIP!

Aslan the Agile Asiatic Lion pounced on Zechariah and decided to have him for supper.

"This stubborn fella never knows when to shut up," Aslan remarked as he gnawed on a meaty zebra bone. "Let's continue planning our escape, shall we?"

MORAL OF THE STORY

You might mean well when offering sensible advice, but if you come across as sanctimonious and preachy, no one is going to listen.

ABOUT
THE AUTHOR

MELANIE LEE is a writer and educator from Singapore.
She is the author of *The Adventures of Squirky the Alien*,
a picture book series which won the Crystal Kite Award
(Middle East/India/Asia division) and Second Prize in the
Samsung KidsTime Authors' Award, both in 2016. Beyond
book publishing, Lee specialises in content related to
arts, heritage, and lifestyle, and has worked with clients
such as the National Museum of Singapore, National Arts
Council and RedMart. She is also Associate Faculty at the
Singapore University of Social Sciences (SUSS) overseeing
media writing courses.

ABOUT
THE ILLUSTRATOR

ARIF RAFHAN is a multi-platform visual artist based in Malaysia and provides services to both corporate and online audiences. He specialises in illustrations, comics and murals. His works can be seen in government and corporate offices, business areas and schools. They are also used by online businesses to promote products.
Arif is a regular live guest artist for events and seminars where he provides live drawings and graphic recordings. When he's not busy with work, he runs doodle classes for the children in his neighbourhood.